This Book Belongs To

DARE YOU!

James Mayhew

Clarion Books
New York

Also by James Mayhew
Katie's Picture Show
Katie and the Dinosaurs
Madame Nightingale Will Sing Tonight
Five Mice and the Moon
(Story by Joyce Dunbar)

Clarion Books
a Houghton Mifflin Company imprint
215 Park Avenue South, New York, NY 10003
Text and illustrations copyright © 1992 by James Mayhew

Published in the United States 1993 by arrangement with
Franklin Watts/Orchard Books
96 Leonard Street, London EC2A 4RH, England.

First published in Great Britain by Orchard Books, 1992

Library of Congress Cataloging-in-Publication Data

Mayhew, James, 1964–
    Dare you! / James Mayhew.
        p.   cm.
    Summary: Susie and Harry find some spooky surprises when they
tiptoe outside in the middle of the night.
    ISBN 0-395-65013-5
    [1. Night—Fiction. 2. Brothers and sisters—Fiction.]
I. Title.
PZ7.M4684Dar   1993
[E]—dc20   92-18862
                                                            CIP
                                                            AC

Printed in Belgium

10 9 8 7 6 5 4 3 2 1

Susie looked up at the moon. It was so bright in the dark night and she felt wide awake.

The light was on in Harry's room. Susie
opened his door.

"I can't sleep," she said.

"I can't either," said Harry. "Let's play
ghosts. That's if you dare."

"All right," said Susie.

Harry and Susie wrapped themselves in
sheets.

"Dare you to turn out the light," said
Harry.

So Susie turned out the light . . .
In the dark the moon was brighter still.

"I'm a better ghost than you are," said
Harry.

"Says who," said Susie.

"Dare you to go downstairs," said Harry.

"Don't make so much noise," hissed Susie.

They stepped on each step as lightly as they could, holding their breath. The last step always creaked, so they left that out altogether.

Downstairs looked different in the dark.
The moon cast shadows on the floor and on
the walls. The clock ticked and its big white
face stared at them.

"Dare you to go outside," said Harry.

"Only if you come," said Susie.

"We could play hide-and-seek," said Harry.

Harry got a chair
and undid the bolt.
Susie found the key and
undid the lock.

They opened the door.
It squeaked and creaked.

"Quiet," said Harry.
"Shhh," said Susie.
"Meow," said
something else . . .

"Did you hear that?"
"It's only the cat."

The cat slipped past Susie into the garden.
The flowers smelt sweet and the moon
covered the garden in a silvery light. Dry
leaves crunched under their feet.

"Dare you to hide,"
said Harry.

"No, you hide, and
I'll seek," said Susie.

"Hoo-hoo!" went
something else . . .

"What was that howl?"
"I think it's an owl."
They watched the owl fly over them, its
pale, silent wings stretched wide.

"Count to a hundred. And no peeping," said Harry. He ran off across the soft grass, and hid in the trees.

The moon went behind a cloud and it was absolutely dark.

"I'm coming, ready or not," called Susie.
"You'll never find me," Harry whispered.
"Flittery-flit," went something else.

"Whatever was that?"
"I think it's a bat!"
The bat fluttered and flapped out of sight.

Susie went to look at the bottom of the garden.

"I can't find you anywhere," she said.

Harry didn't say a word.

The garden was silent. Harry couldn't see
Susie any more. It was too dark. 'What if she
never finds me?' he thought.

"Hurry up, Susie,"
Harry whispered.
Susie didn't answer.

"Susie, where are you?"
said Harry, coming out
of the shadows.

He could hear footsteps.
Were they in front,
or were they behind?
Was it the cat?
Or the owl?
Or a bat?

The moon came out.
Harry saw a strange white shape in front of him!

"Whooo!" wailed Susie.

"Oh, it's *you!*" said Harry.

"I was here all the time," said Susie. "And you were scared."

"Well, you screamed," said Harry.

"I never did," said Susie. "Anyway, I'm
going back to bed now."

"Good, I'm fed up with playing ghosts,"
said Harry.

They went back together through the trees, and the branches pulled at their hair. Spiders' webs tickled their faces. Thorns tugged at the sheets.

Harry stopped. "Listen! What's that sound?"
"You're just trying to scare me," said Susie.

From somewhere in front – or was it behind? – voices in the shadows called out.

But it wasn't the cat,
or an owl,
or a bat!
Harry and Susie screamed. "GHOSTS!"
They dropped the sheets and ran. The ghosts
swept towards them, reaching out their pale
arms . . .

"What on earth are you doing out here?"
said one.
   "You're making enough noise to wake the
whole street!" said the other.

"Mum!" said Susie.

"Dad!" said Harry. "We thought you were ghosts!"

"You shouldn't be out in the dark," said Mum.

"Why not, I wasn't scared," said Harry.

"Neither was I," said Susie.

"Well, we were," said Dad. "We didn't know where you were."

"I was a little bit scared," said Susie.

"Me too," said Harry.

"Don't do it again," said Mum, turning off the light.

Susie lay awake and listened.
But she couldn't hear anything . . .
Not the cat,
or the owl,
or the bat.
She could just see the moon, so bright in the
still, clear night.